Let's go on an adventure!

The
Adventures of
Black Dog

Beached Whale

Tiffany Schmidt &

By TIFFANY SCHMIDT

Illustrated By ANDREW THEOPHILOPOULOS

ADAPTIVE BOOKS

An Imprint of Adaptive Studios
Culver City, CA
www.adaptivestudios.com

The sea at Vineyard Haven talks,
It's more than waves against the rocks.

Shhh, listen carefully you'll hear,
Adventures, rescues, buccaneers . . .

It always starts in the same way
and ends when Black Dog saves the day.

A bottle with a message inside,
Washes up in the harbor's tide.

Hear it CLINK against the rocks!
Seagull brings it to the docks.
Black Dog sees him flying near.
Captain joins her on the pier.

The note says Whale is in some trouble.

Black Dog leaps up on the double.

Bark! Bark! Bark! "Let's go and help!"
Her message spreads from fish to kelp.

Black Dog, Captain, Tess, and Jack
Call to the shore,
"We'll be back."

From the Shenandoah's bow
Black Dog barks, "We're coming now!"

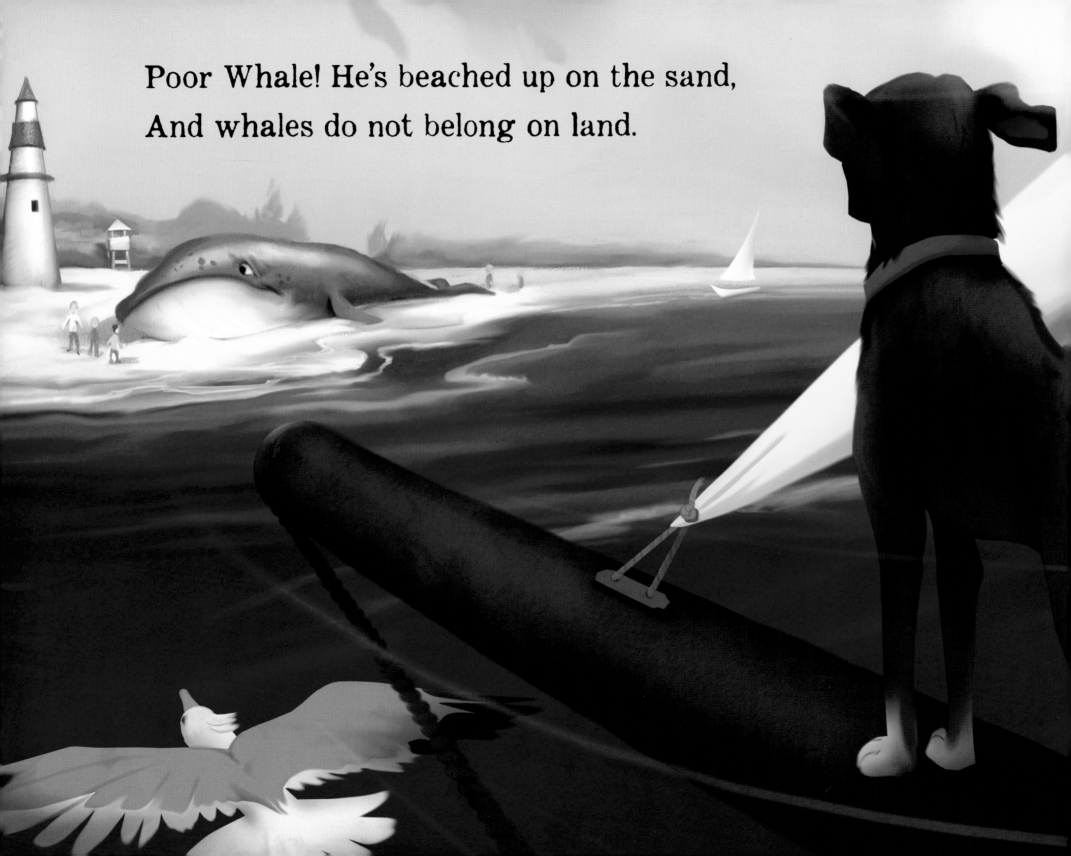

Poor Whale! He's beached up on the sand,
And whales do not belong on land.

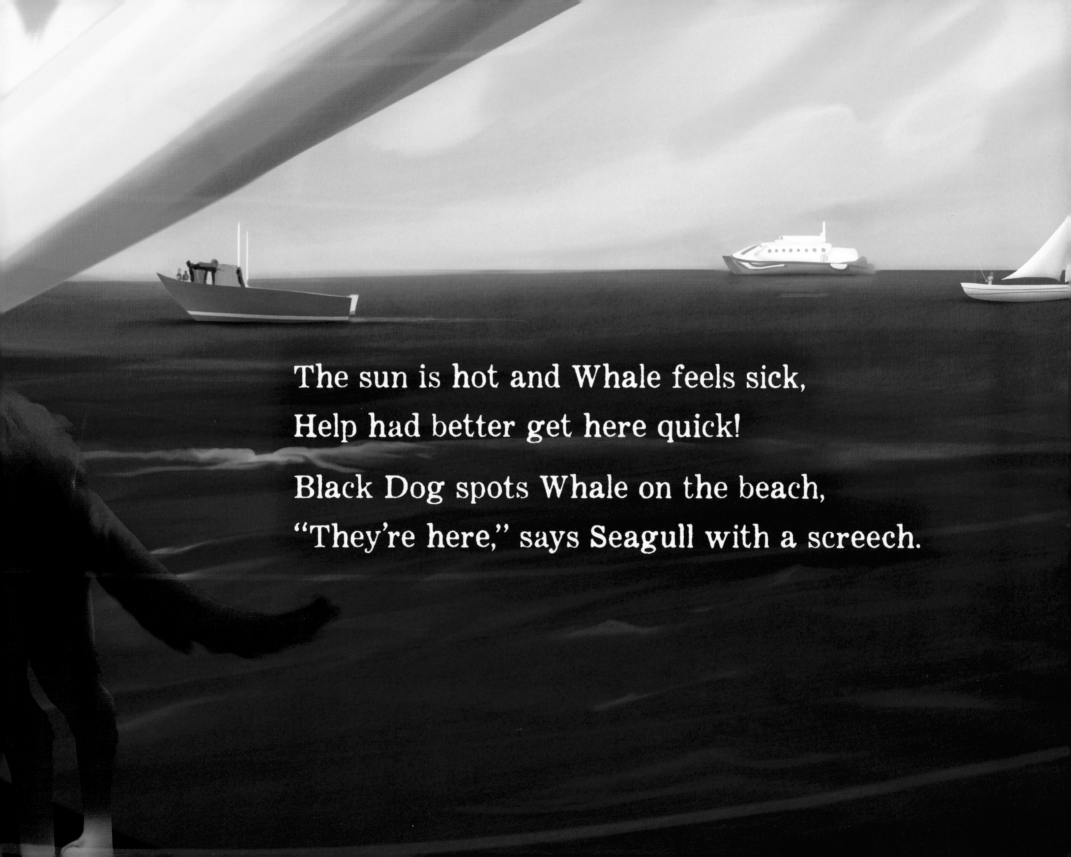

The sun is hot and Whale feels sick,
Help had better get here quick!

Black Dog spots Whale on the beach,
"They're here," says Seagull with a screech.

They drop their anchor through a wave.

"We'll help you, Whale.
You must be brave!"

Jack pours buckets full of water
To cool down Whale as it gets hotter.

Tess hands Captain ropes to tie.
Black Dog gives it her best try.

The ropes are wrapped around Whale's tail,
Black Dog knows they will not fail.

Jack tells the crew, "We're almost ready!
Here we go now. Hold us steady."

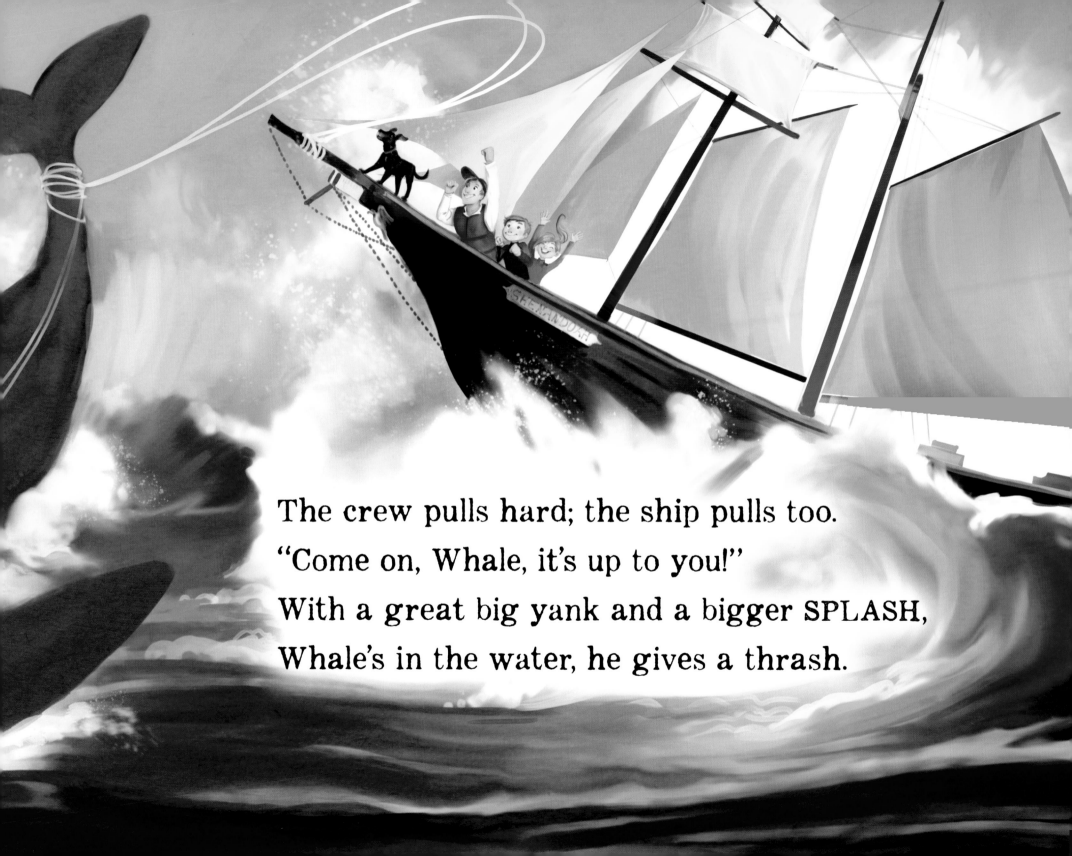

The crew pulls hard; the ship pulls too.
"Come on, Whale, it's up to you!"
With a great big yank and a bigger SPLASH,
Whale's in the water, he gives a thrash.

Whale waves his tail
and spouts, "HOORAY!
The Shenandoah saves
the day!"

"Thank you, Black Dog, and your crew,
I owe my safety all to you.

Next time I'm swimming near the shore,
I'll keep an eye on the ocean floor."

With a last tail-wave and a great big SPLISH,
Whale dives down to greet some fish.

Black Dog stands proudly on the ship,
Bark! Bark! "What a helpful trip."

So if you're ever far up north,
And find your way to Black Dog Wharf,

Listen to the Vineyard Haven Sound.
Endless adventures will be found.

Black Dog, Captain, and the schooner's crew
Will go on other journeys, too.

To my Schmidtlets—
may you go on many adventures and find many friends.
—T.S.

Text copyright, jacket art, and interior illustrations © 2014
Adaptive Studios Inc. and Black Dog Tavern Company, Inc.
All rights reserved
Additional concepts and artwork by Betsy Bauer
Published in the United States by Adaptive Books, an imprint of Adaptive Studios

Visit us on the web at www.adaptivestudios.com

Library of Congress Cataloging-in-Publication Data
Schmidt, Tiffany.
Adventures of Black Dog – Beached Whale / by Tiffany Schmidt ; illustrated by Andrew Theophilopoulos – 1st ed.

ISBN 978-0-9960666-1-7 (hardcover)

Printed in South Korea

[1. Juvenile Fiction / Action & Adventure / General] [2. Juvenile Fiction / Animals / Dogs] [3. Juvenile Fiction / Social Issues / Friendship]
[4. Nature / Animals / Marine Life] [TRAVEL / United States / Northeast / New England (CT, MA, ME, NH, RI, VT)]

Book design by Torborg Davern

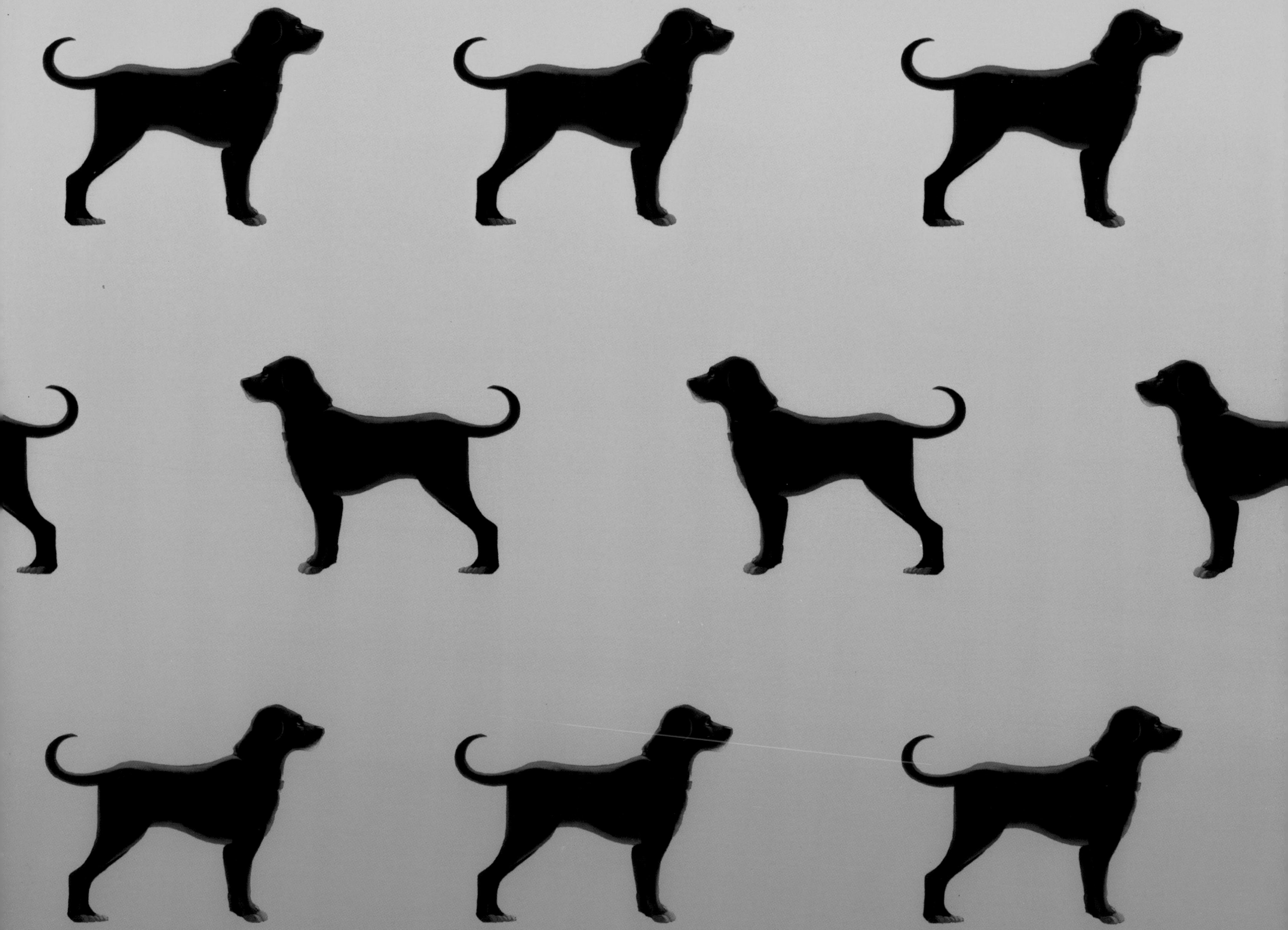